DATE DUE

AP 12 '02			
NO 03 '03			

DEMCO 38-297

Making Their Mark: Women in Science and Medicine™

Jane Goodall
Leading Animal Behaviorist

Liza N. Burby

Hammer

The Rosen Publishing Group's
PowerKids Press™
New York

Published in 1997 by The Rosen Publishing Group, Inc.
29 East 21st Street, New York, NY 10010

First Edition

Book Design: Erin McKenna

Photo credits: pp. 4, 12 © Camerique/H. Armstrong Roberts, Inc.; p. 7 by Carrie Ann Grippo; pp. 11, 19 © AP/Wide World Photos; p. 15 © Fotos International/Archive Photos; p. 16 © Von Hoffmann/H. Armstrong Roberts, Inc.; p. 20 © Wide World Photos, Inc.

Burby, Liza N.
    Jane Goodall / by Liza N. Burby
        p.   cm. — (Making their mark)
    Includes index.
    Summary: A simple presentation of the life of the ethologist who brought chimp behavior to the attention of the world.
    ISBN 0-8239-5025-5 (library bound)
    1. Goodall, Jane, 1934– —Juvenile literature. 2. Primatologists—England—Biography—Juvenile literature. 3. Women primatologists—England—Biography—Juvenile literature. [1. Goodall, Jane, 1934– . 2. Ethologists. 3. Women—Biography.] I. Title. II. Series: Burby, Liza N. Making their mark.
QL31.G58B87 1996
591'.092—dc20
[B]
                                96–41730
                                CIP
                                AC

Manufactured in the United States of America

Contents

Hidden in the Hay

When Jane Goodall was five years old, she wanted to know how an egg came out of a hen. So she hid in the chicken coop for five hours. When she finally saw an egg roll out from under the hen's feathers, Jane was excited. She ran to tell her mother. Her mother was worried. She had been looking for Jane for hours. But she did not get angry. She was pleased to learn of Jane's interest and **encouraged** (en-KER-ijd) her to study animals.

◀ Some of the first animals that Jane was interested in were the chickens in her family's chicken coop.

A Love of Animals

Jane was born in London, England, on August 3, 1934. As a little girl she loved all animals. One of her favorites was a dog named Rusty. Jane taught him tricks. She learned a lot about animal **behavior** (bee-HAYV-yor) from Rusty. She also enjoyed reading books like *The Story of Doctor Doolittle*, which is about a man who could talk to animals. When Jane was seven, she decided that some day she would go to Africa to learn the secrets of wild animals. She knew that nothing would stop her.

You can learn about animals from spending time with them. ▶

AFRICA

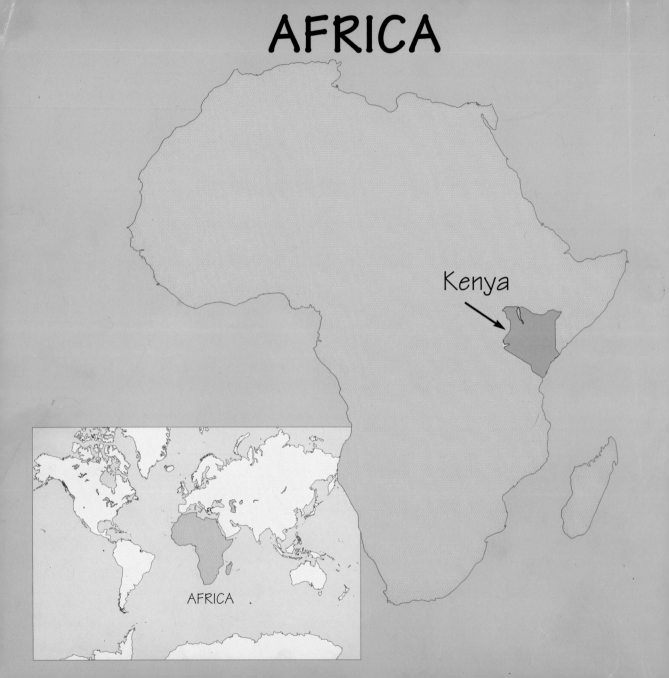

Kenya

AFRICA

Waiting for Her Chance

Jane had many different jobs after she finished high school. She worked as a secretary, a filmmaker, and a waitress. Her mother did not have enough money to send her to college. But Jane did not give up her dreams. Jane waited for the chance to go to Africa to learn about wild animals. One day that chance came. A friend invited her to visit her family's home in Kenya, Africa.

◀ Jane's dream of traveling to Africa came true.

Talking to Animals

Jane decided to stay in Africa. There she met Louis Leakey, a famous **scientist** (SY-en-tist) who was interested in animals and the first **human beings** (HYOO-man BEE-ingz). Jane worked with him. Her job included digging for **fossils** (FOS-sils) and caring for **orphaned** (OR-fand) wild animals. After a while, Jane knew what she wanted to do with her life. She wanted to live where the wild animals lived and learn all about them. She wanted to talk to the animals, just like Doctor Doolittle.

After being in Africa, Jane knew that she wanted ▶ to spend her life studying wild animals.

Finding a Way

Sometimes Louis Leakey spoke to Jane about chimpanzees. He said that they are the animals that are most like humans. He thought that learning more about them might help people understand how our **ancestors** (AN-ses-terz) lived long ago. Jane wanted to study them. Since she had not gone to college, she had not been trained. But when she asked Louis if she could study them, he told her they would find a way.

◄ Chimpanzees are animals that are closely related to humans.

13

Studying Chimpanzees

Jane went to college to become an **ethologist** (eeth-OL-uh-jist), a person who studies how animals live and **behave** (be-HAYV). In 1960, at age 26, she traveled to another part of Africa. She set up a tent in Gombe National Park, near the country of Zaire. At last, she was going to learn the secrets of wildlife in Africa. Louis had warned her that it would take a very long time to learn about chimpanzees. Jane didn't care how long it took.

Jane watched the chimps carefully, studying their behavior. ▶

Hiding in the Jungle

For almost a year, Jane hid in the jungle and watched chimpanzees. No one had ever studied animals in this way before. Jane learned many interesting things while she watched. She learned that chimpanzees are like humans. They **imitate** (IM-ih-tayt) each other, which is something other animals cannot do. Chimpanzees can feel happy, sad, angry, and scared. They kiss, punch, play, and cry. They even make 30 different sounds.

◀ Chimps have feelings, make sounds, and can solve certain problems.

The Chimps' New Friend

As the chimpanzees got used to Jane, many became her friends. She met chimp families and watched how they cared for each other. She learned how smart they are. She saw that chimps can make tools out of things like sticks. This was an exciting discovery, because everyone had believed that only people could make tools. Like humans, chimps can plan ahead what they will do. They can also solve certain problems.

Many of the animals that Jane studied became her friends. ▶

18

Saving the Chimps

Jane learned more about chimpanzees than anyone else ever had. She believed in herself and did not let anything get in her way. She used this **courage** (KER-ej) in helping chimps. She learned that the number of chimps was getting smaller. The **rain forests** (RAYN FOR-ests) in which the chimps live are being destroyed by humans. Jane knew that it was important to save the chimps. She set up three parks where chimps can live safely.

◀ Jane dedicated her life to saving chimpanzees.

Roots & Shoots

Today Jane travels all over the world. She asks young people to help save the **environment** (en-VY-ron-ment) for all living things. She has a program called Roots & Shoots. Through Roots & Shoots, kids can learn more about the environment and how to help it. They can also do important things, such as recycle, clean up parks, and learn about animals. Jane teaches people that by working together, we can make the world a better place for animals and humans.

Glossary

ancestor (AN-ses-ter) People in our family who lived before us.

behave (bee-HAYV) How someone acts.

behavior (bee-HAYV-yor) The way someone acts.

courage (KER-ej) Being brave.

encourage (en-KER-ij) Give support to.

environment (en-VY-ron-ment) The place and way in which humans, animals, and plants live.

ethologist (eeth-OL-uh-jist) A person who studies how animals live and behave.

fossil (FOS-sil) The remains of a very old plant or animal.

human being (HYOO-man BEE-ing) Person.

imitate (IM-ih-tayt) To copy what someone does.

orphaned (OR-fand) An animal that does not have a living mother or father.

rain forest (RAYN FOR-est) A very wet area that has many kinds of plants, trees, and animals.

scientist (SY-en-tist) A person who studies the way things are and act in the universe.

23

Index